THE GIRL AND THE GOATHERD
OR
THIS AND THAT
AND
THUS AND SO

WRITTEN AND ILLUSTRATED BY

EVALINE NESS

The goatherd wanted the ugliest girl in the world to marry him, but the ugliest girl wasn't interested. All she could think of was being beautiful.

How the girl becomes beautiful—and what happens then—is conjured up in a fantasy romp involving the goatherd, a witch, lots of goats, many birds' eggs, and—this and that and thus and so.

In Miss Ness's first book written and illustrated by her since the Caldecott-winning *Sam, Bangs & Moonshine* in 1967, she combines a sharp wit with a tender understanding of human nature. This picture book is rich in illustration, deft humor, and warmth.

THE GIRL AND THE GOATHERD

THE
GIRL AND THE GOATHERD
OR
THIS AND THAT
AND
THUS AND SO

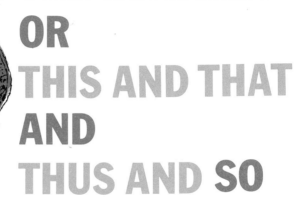

WRITTEN AND ILLUSTRATED BY **EVALINE NESS**

E. P. DUTTON & CO., INC. NEW YORK

Other Books by Evaline Ness

MR. MIACCA

SAM, BANGS & MOONSHINE

23061

Published simultaneously in Canada by Clarke,
Irwin & Company Limited, Toronto and Vancouver

SBN: 0-525-30657-9 (Trade)   SBN: 0-525-30658-7 (DLLB)
Library of Congress Catalog Card Number: 72-116885

Printed in the U.S.A.
First Edition

To my sister Josephine

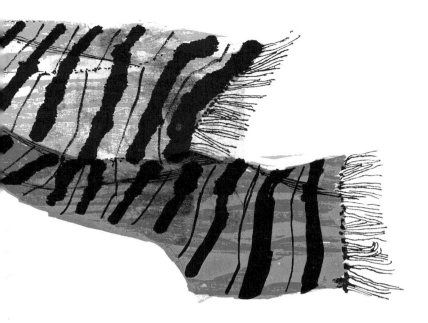

There was once a girl and she was ugly. And she did fret and droop because she was not beautiful.

Well, the girl got uglier as she got older, and when it came time for her to marry, no man except the goatherd would look at her. And he did ask her for her hand.

But the girl, she could think of nought else except to be beautiful. So she turned the goatherd away.

Now there came a day as the girl sat a-moping that a witch appeared before her.

"What a sight you be! The ugliest girl in the land," said the witch. "But I'll make you the most beautiful of all if you do as I bid."

"Ooooooooo?" asked the girl.

"Yes," said the witch. "I want a roof to my house made of tender oak saplings, and I want my roof done, come dawn."

Well now, the only place to find tender oak saplings was on the top of the highest hill. So the girl started out at a mighty pace. Up the hill she went and down the hill, up the hill and down the hill she floundered, fetching the tender oak saplings. But come midnight, she hadn't near enough for a roof to the witch's house. So the girl, she just stood and boo-hooed.

Then along came the goatherd and asked, "What ails you?"

"Ooooooo," wailed the girl. "The most beautiful of all I'll not be, come dawn, if I've not done the witch's roof with these saplings."

Said the goatherd, "I like your looks the way they be, but don't fret yourself, I'll help you."

So saying, the goatherd did blast his horn and all his goats came clopping to his side and followed him up the hill. And down they came saddled with tender oak saplings— enough to cover *forty* witches' houses.

Well, the girl and the goatherd snipped, snapped, and stacked; bent and wattled those saplings all night. Come dawn, they'd built up a roof to the witch's house like nobody had ever laid eyes on before.

Then the girl, all smiles and hardly a thank-you for the goatherd, knocked on the witch's door. The witch gave her a glare and came out to see her roof.

Meantime, the girl hopped from one foot to the other, so eager was she to be told she was the most beautiful of all. But the witch eyed her up and down and said: "You're better to look at than before, but beautiful you're not."

"Ooooooo!" cried the girl. She was that disappointed.

"Hark you now," said the witch. "Go fetch me a hundred yards of cobwebs for curtains to my windows. And I want them, come dawn."

Well, that girl, she sat herself down and sniveled, for how could she ever find a hundred yards of cobwebs!

Then along happened the goatherd and he asked, "What ails you now, then?"

"Ooooooo!" bawled the girl. "The most beautiful of all I'll not be, come dawn, if I've not found a hundred yards of cobwebs for curtains to the witch's windows."

"I like your looks the way they be," said the goatherd. "But don't naggle yourself. I'll help you."

So he called his goats and took his shears and cut away their long silky hair. And while he sheared, the girl did spin, and when she'd spun, she threaded up her bobbins and whirred. They never stopped the whole night through. Come dawn, with this and that and thus and so, they'd a hundred yards of lace, fine as cobwebs, the like to make a spider jealous.

Without a good-by or a thank-you, the girl grabbed up the lace and ran to the witch, who snatched the stuff and said to the girl: "You are more beautiful now than some, but not the most. But if you do as I bid one more time, you will be the most beautiful of all. Get to the wood and steal a thousand birds' eggs and bring them to me, come dawn."

Law! That girl had no hankering to steal, but she did hanker after being the most beautiful of all, so she ran to the wood and up the trees she scrambled and down the trees. Up and down, up and down filching birds' eggs right and left, but come midnight, she had nowhere near a thousand of them, so she let out a moan.

Then along came the goatherd. "What ails you, then?" asked he.

"Ooooooooo," whined the girl. "The most beautiful of all I'll not be, come dawn, if I've not a thousand birds' eggs and I've nowhere near that many."

Said the goatherd, "I like your looks the way they be, but don't addle yourself. I'll help you."

Whereupon, he took his rope and wove a stout ladder that joined the trees one to another. Then the two set to and picked and plucked and never paused the whole night long. Come dawn, they'd a thousand eggs betwixt them.

Then off the girl buzzed to the witch with the eggs and never a nod to the goatherd. While the witch counted up the eggs, the girl hummed and fluttered and twittered and wiggled, she was that a-gog to be the most beautiful of all.

At last the witch gave the girl a sneer and said, "You've got your wish. Take a look in the well."

And sure enough, the girl had become the most beautiful of all.

It didn't take but a day for the news of her beauty to fly through the land. The old king called her to his castle and he set her down with his gems and treasures. Knights and lords and princes and kings came from far and wide to eye her. But not one spoke to her or touched her or even smiled on her. They thought, you know, she was more gold than girl.

23061

The very next thing, that girl took up with her snuffling and sighing again and she drooped more than ever before. She felt that dismal.

Suddenly she heard: "*Now* what ails you?" And there stood the goatherd.

"Ooooooo!" sobbed the girl. "I'm done. To be the most beautiful of all's not the first and last to be happy. I'd sooner be ugly."

"I like you no matter what your looks be," said the goatherd. "But if you'll stop your nattering and marry me, I'll help you."

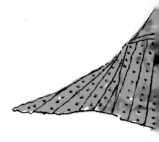

So right off, the girl and the goatherd ran to the witch's house and set to work.

What a bustle! Back went the birds' eggs all to their nests. Down came the curtains of cobwebby lace, and then stitched by the girl to a wedding-dress veil. Off went the tender oak-sapling roof, which the goatherd carted away to top his own house.

And with this and that and thus and so, betwixt them together they worked the night through. And then they got married, come dawn.

EVALINE NESS was raised in Pontiac, Michigan, and she began her art studies at the Art Institute of Chicago at the age of nineteen. She subsequently studied at the Corcoran School of Art in Washington, D.C., the Accademia de Belle Arti in Rome, and the Art Students' League in New York City. Miss Ness began illustrating juveniles in 1960, after a successful career as a commercial artist. Twice runner-up for the Caldecott Medal, she received the award in 1967 for *Sam, Bangs & Moonshine*.

ABOUT THE STORY: The development of *The Girl and the Goatherd* is best explained by the author. "The colloquial tone of the story evolves from nostalgia for a particular period of my childhood. Every summer my mother took me to her parents' farm near Willis, Virginia. I was allowed to wander freely and eventually I found an ancient, scraggly lady who lived in a hut in the hills. We became friends and spent many afternoons in her riotous flower garden discussing everything. (She did all the talking.) I remember nothing that we discussed. I remember clearly the *way* she discussed."

ABOUT THE ART: The artwork is mixed media. Straightforward pen-and-ink drawings are used for the subject matter. The backgrounds are textures lifted from surfaces with inking and spoon rubbings as in woodcuts. The author-illustrator adds: "Now and then there *are* woodcuts." The display type is set in Franklin Gothic Condensed and the text initial letters in Neuland; the text type is set in Janson. The three-color art is preseparated and the book is printed by offset.

DATE DUE

FEB 15 '74	JUL 27 '84		
MAR 12 '74	OCT. 6 1987		
MAR 29 '74	AUG 24 '90		
APR 16 '74	NOV 21 '91		
MAY 3 '74	AUG 28 '95		
MAY 10 '74	AUG 8 '00		
MAY 24 '74			
JUL 3 '74			
AUG 5 '74			
SEP 5 '74			
DEC 23 '74			
APR 1 '75			
MAY 12 '75			
SEP 11 '75			
NOV 10 '77			
MAR 10 '78			
APR 19 '78			
DEC 6 '83			